First published in 2013 by Pont Books, an imprint of
Gomer Press, Llandysul, Ceredigion, SA44 4JL

ISBN 978 1 84851 711 0

A CIP record for this title is available from the British Library.

This book is published with the financial support of the
Welsh Books Council.

Printed and bound in Wales at
Gomer Press, Llandysul, Ceredigion

EAT UP, EMLYN!

ANGELA MORRIS

Emlyn was a tiny baby.
His brother Emrys was big and strong.

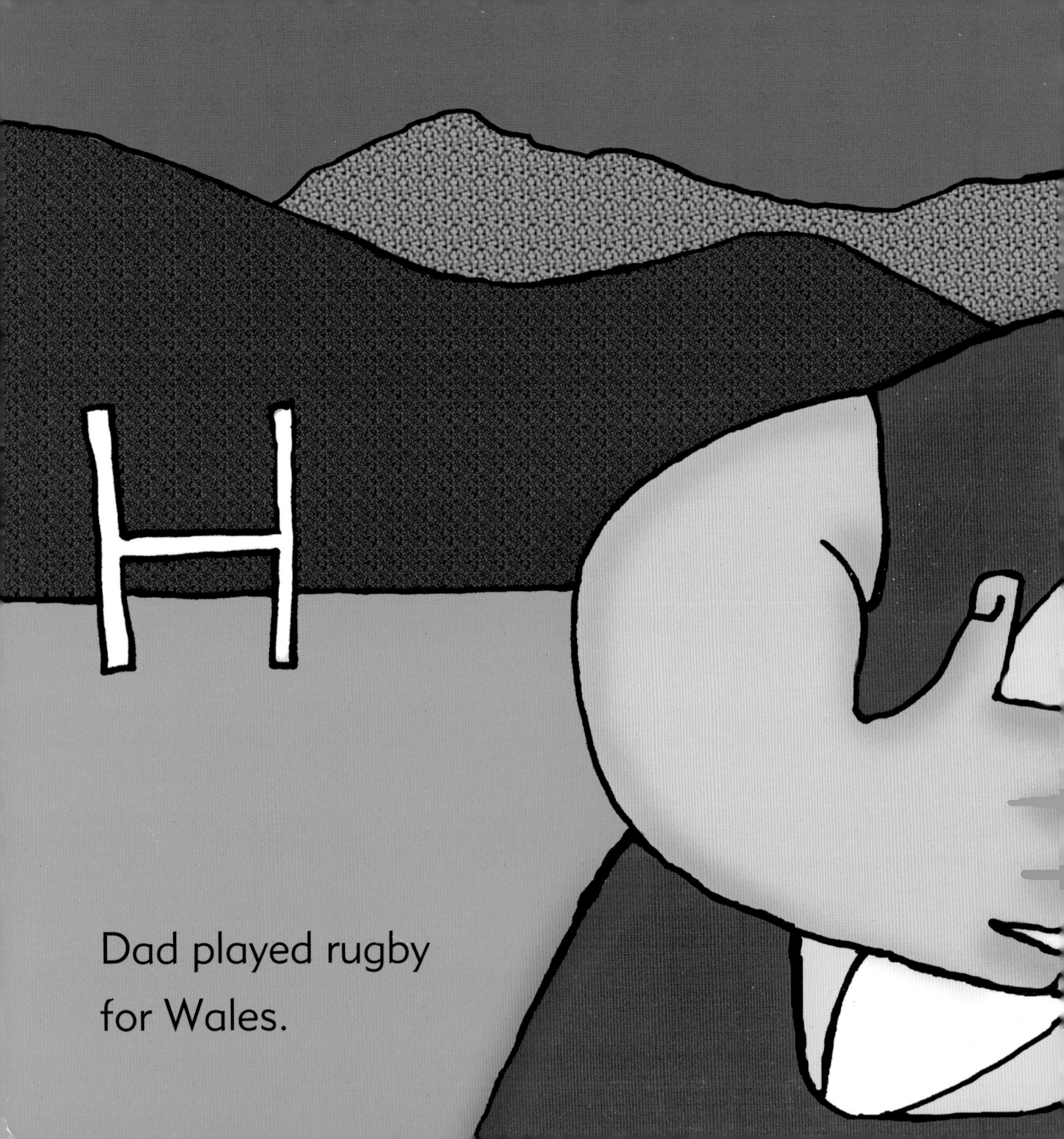

Dad played rugby
for Wales.

But Mum was worried.

'This baby's getting smaller,' she said.

'He won't drink his milk . . .

. . . or eat his food.'

'Eat up, Emlyn,'
said Emrys.

Guto offered to share his bone.

But Emlyn just wasn't interested.

'I've had enough of this,' said Mum.

'We're going to see Nain.'
Evans

'Try Emlyn with my *cawl,*' said Nain.
'It's full of good things.'

philly cheese
cawl

Emlyn wasn't sure at first . . .

but then he tasted it. 'Yum!'

He grew . . .

bigger . . .

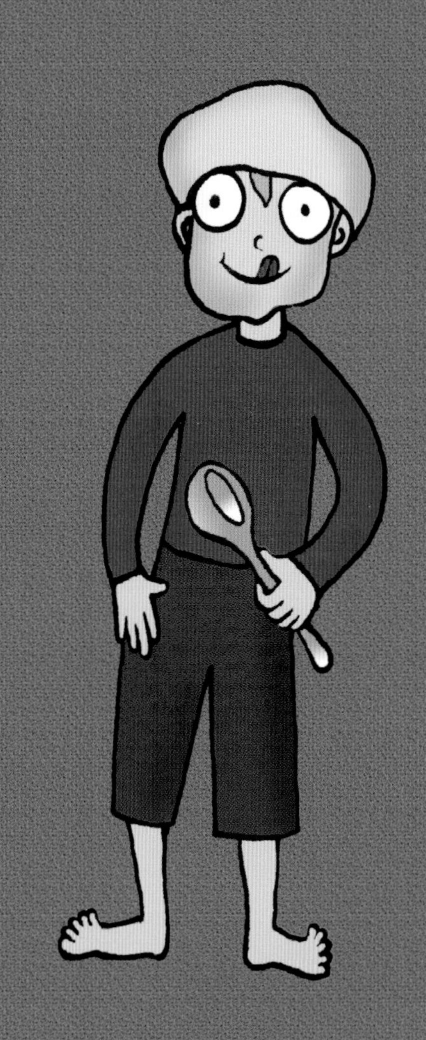

and bigger . . .

and bigger . . .

Soon he was big enough

to play rugby with Dad and Emrys.

Soon he was big enough

to play rugby for Wales.

Nain's *cawl* became famous . . .

and so did Nain!

Her *cawl* won prizes . . .
And so did Emlyn.

'*Diolch*, Nain.'
Nain's Cawl